Blast Off!

Malachy Doyle

Illustrated by
Gill McLean

QED Publishing

The toys have found an empty spaceship.

"Hey!" yelled Rocco Rabbit. "I could be the first bunny in space!"

"But there's only room for one of us inside," said Emily Elephant. "Who's it going to be?"

"Oh dear!" sighed Jim Giraffe.
"I think I'm a bit too tall!
I'd better stay down here."

"I'm not! And I'm not too
small, either!" shouted Rocco.

10...

"Is there anyone else who might not want to go?"
asked Lenny Lion. "It's best to decide now."

"It looks a bit of a squeeze!" said Emily Elephant.
"I think I'll stay with Jim."

9...

As Emily turned away, her trunk
caught on the light switch.

"BAAAAAAA!"

"Scared of the dark, Sally Sheep?"
asked Patricia Pig. "I think you'd be
happier at home with Emily and Jim."

"Rabbits live in holes.
We're used to the dark!"
said Rocco.

8...

"Maybe you'd better stay here too, Chickadoodle," said Henry Horse. "You're a bit little to be flying off on your own."

"OK!" replied the shy little chick.

"Hey!" called Rocco. "I'm not the smallest after all!
Maybe I've got a chance!"

7...

There were only six animals left.
They climbed up on top of the wardrobe.

"Does everyone like being up so high?"
asked Martha Monkey.

"Not me!" groaned Lenny Lion. "I just like prowling through the grass!"

6...

"Don't forget
to open your
parachutes
everyone!"
cried Rocco.

"I think you'd be happier on the ground, Patricia," said Henry Horse.

"I think you're right," grunted Patricia.

5...

"OK, there's only four of us now," said Barney
Bulldog. "Let's see who's fit enough to fly!"

"Fit as a flea!"

"This is fun!"

"I'm a good hopper!"

"Count me out!
I've had enough!"
moaned Henry.

4...

"So – it's just us three now," said Barney.
"Who can get through the Mystery Maze?
We don't want anyone getting lost in space!"

"I love digging!"
exclaimed Rocco.

"So now there's only you and me!" said Rocco.
"Do you like aliens?"

"Not at all!" yapped Barney.

"They don't scare me!" said Rocco.

2...

"Well done, Rocco!" cried Barney.
"You're going to be an astro-bunny!"

"Woo-hay!" yelled Rocco.

Woo-hay!

1...

Blast off!

Notes for parents and teachers

- Look at the cover and pictures in the book before reading it to the children. Can they think what the story is about?

- Ask the children to find out as much as they can about spaceships and space travel. Have any real animals ever flown into space? When did the first person land on the Moon?

- If the children were the ones who had to choose who could go up in a spaceship, how would they decide? What do they think people need to know, if they're going to fly in space. What would people need to be like?

- Can the children find a word to describe each of the characters in the story? For example, they might say Rocco Rabbit is brave.

- Can the children count down from ten to one backwards? They can finish their countdown with the words "Blast off!" Can they count down from twenty to one?

- Encourage them to think of an animal beginning with the letter A, and then try to think of one for as many letters of the alphabet as they can. Then ask them to give each of the creatures a name that starts with the same letter, e.g. Adam Ant, Rocco Rabbit. They could draw a picture of each one, with their name underneath.

- What do they think happened after the book ended? Ask them to tell the story of Rocco's journey into space. Where did he go? What did he see? Who did he meet? How did he get home again?

Editor: Alexandra Koken
Designer: Chris Fraser

Copyright © QED Publishing 2011

This edition published 2012 for Index Books

First published in the UK in 2011 by QED Publishing
A Quarto Group company
230 City Road
London EC1V 2TT
www.qed-publishing.co.uk

A catalogue record for this book is available from the British Library.

ISBN 978 1 84835 753 2

Printed in China